P9-CAB-958

STAR WARS™

LEIA AND THE GREAT ISLAND ESCAPE

ADAPTED BY **JASON FRY**

BASED ON **MOVING TARGET** BY CECIL CASTELLUCCI & JASON FRY

ILLUSTRATED BY **PILOT STUDIO**

© & TM 2016 Lucasfilm Ltd. All rights reserved. Published by Disney • Lucasfilm Press, an imprint of Disney Book Group. No part of this book may be reproduced or transmitted in any form or by any means, electronic or mechanical, including photocopying, recording, or by any information storage and retrieval system, without written permission from the publisher. For information address Disney • Lucasfilm Press, 1101 Flower Street, Glendale, California 91201.

Printed in the United States of America

First Paperback Edition, December 2016

1 3 5 7 9 10 8 6 4 2

Library of Congress Control Number on file

FAC-029261-16302

ISBN 978-1-368-00240-0

Visit the official *Star Wars* website at: www.starwars.com.

DISNEP
LUCASFILM
PRESS

WITHDRAWN

LOS ANGELES · NEW YORK

PRINCESS LEIA ORGANA WAS ON A SECRET MISSION.

She was leading Imperial ships on a great space chase across the galaxy.

Leia needed to distract the Empire so the Rebel Alliance could prepare for war.

The next stop on her mission was the volcanic island planet of Sesid.

Ace pilot Nien Nunb, veteran commando Lokmarcha, communications specialist Kidi, and demolitions expert Antrot accompanied Leia.

Aboard Nien's ship, the *Mellcrawler*, the team touched down on a giant lily pad. Leia planned to meet a mysterious freedom fighter known as Captain Aurelant on Sesid. They hoped Aurelant could help them distract the Empire and would perhaps even join the Rebellion.

In town, Leia and her friends tried to blend in with the island tourists, but there was no time for fun. They had work to do!

While Nien stayed with the ship, Leia and the rest of the team boarded a boat. They skimmed across the waves toward a nearby island, where they would meet Aurelant and send out a beacon to attract the Empire.

When they reached the island, Lokmarcha led Kidi and Antrot to the top of a volcano to activate the beacon while Leia waited for Aurelant on the black-sand beach below.

Hours passed with no sign of Aurelant. The team decided to return to the *Mellcrawler*. Antrot was relieved; he had been worried that the volcano would erupt. Lokmarcha explained that there were tall, black escape pods all over the island in case of emergency.

But as Leia looked out across the water, it became clear that an active volcano was the least of their worries. . . .

The beacon had worked! Stormtroopers were streaking along the surface of the ocean on waveskimmers and firing at the team of rebels.

Leia opened the throttle, sending their boat hurtling across the waves, while Lokmarcha fired at the Imperials.

As Leia veered their boat side to side to avoid enemy fire, Kidi alerted Nien to take off and await further instructions. Leia told Antrot to arm detonators and throw them into the water to slow down the troopers.

But Antrot's detonators were no match for the Imperials, and the rebels were soon surrounded.

It was only a matter of time before their boat had been blasted.

Smoke began to pour from their damaged vessel as the waveskimmers drew closer. Leia scanned the horizon, hoping to find an island they could reach before their boat sank into the ocean.

Suddenly, a massive shadow appeared in the water beneath them!

When the shadow broke the surface, Leia saw that it was a submarine vehicle dripping with shaggy seaweed.

The strange vessel opened like a huge mouth and swallowed the team's boat whole before sinking back beneath the waves. The rebels couldn't tell if they were being rescued or captured.

Inside, aliens with red eyes and sharp teeth surrounded the team, brandishing blasters and knives as they took away the rebels' weapons. They were Draedan pirates, and they easily outnumbered Leia and her crew.

Then a massive tattooed Draedan pushed through the crowd and stood right in front of Leia. The princess held her ground, but the other rebels were sure they had been defeated . . .

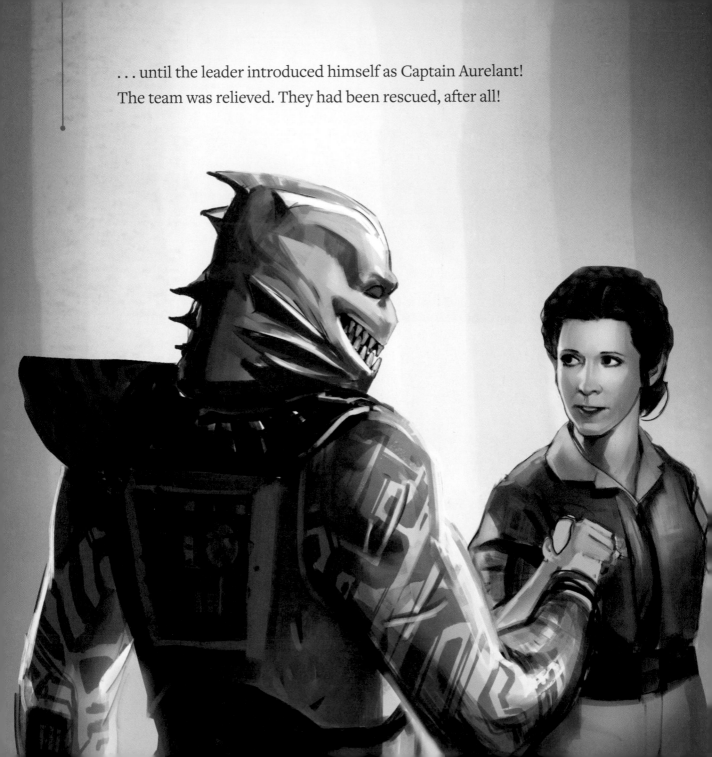

. . . until the leader introduced himself as Captain Aurelant!
The team was relieved. They had been rescued, after all!

Leia contacted Nien, who was equally glad to hear that his team was all right. But he informed Leia that they needed to get off the island, and fast! An Imperial Star Destroyer was lurking above Sesid, and there were more on the way.

Leia had no idea how they would rendezvous with Nien and the *Mellcrawler*, but Aurelant had a plan.

It turned out the escape pods on the volcanic islands *would* come in handy. As the team boarded one of the pods, Aurelant promised to have his friends release escape pods all over Sesid so the Empire wouldn't be able to tell which one held the rebels. Leia thanked Aurelant for his help, and moments later their pod rocketed away!

All across Sesid, escape pods shot into the sky. Puzzled stormtroopers and Imperial officers watched as hundreds of pods rocketed toward space, leaving bright streaks behind them.

Nien homed in on Leia's comlink signal and retrieved the team.

Back on board the *Mellcrawler*, the rebels celebrated another successful mission. But their job was far from over.

If there was any hope of defeating the Empire, Leia needed to keep the Imperials distracted by remaining a moving target.

The great space chase would continue!